Score One More

Marilyn Janovitz

I Like to Read®

HOLIDAY HOUSE • NEW YORK

"They say May can't play," says Pen.

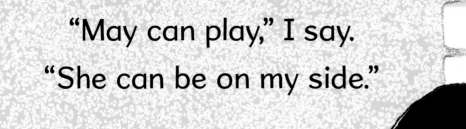

"May can play," I say.
"She can be on my side."

Lin kicks the ball.

They run.

They pass.

We block. But we do not get the ball.

Lin kicks again.

She gets it in.
"Score!" they yell.

I have the ball.

I score!

The score is 1 to 1.

They take the ball.

We get it back.

I need to score one more.

It is up to me.

May yells, "Kick it in, Sam!"

But I pass the ball to May.

I will let her try.

May kicks.

May scores!

We win!